Sisters stick together

"What do you guys think you're doing?" Caroline squawked.

Patricia unzipped her backpack and showed Caroline all the dollar bills she had collected. "Selling your flower seeds," she said proudly. "Everybody who bought a chance on the shopping spree at We-Love-Toys got a pack of seeds, too."

"But who's going to pay a hundred dollars to the toy store for the shopping spree?" Caroline asked.

"You mean *we* have to pay for it?" Vicki began to chew her bottom lip the way she always did when she was about to cry.

Caroline put her arms around her youngest sister. "Don't worry, Vicki. I'll think of something."

"We might as well need a *million* dollars." Patricia sank to the ground in a heap. "We were only trying to help you. . . ."

"Yeah," Vicki said. "We sold all your seed packs."

"*All* of them?" Caroline felt a huge lump in her throat, and her eyes filled with tears. Since her sisters had done so much for her, she *had* to figure out a way to solve their problem. "I said I'd think of something, and I will. I promise."

Look for these books in the Caroline Zucker series:

Caroline Zucker
Helps Out

by Jan Bradford
Illustrated by Marcy Ramsey

Troll Associates

Library of Congress Cataloging-in-Publication Data

Bradford, Jan.
  Caroline Zucker helps out / by Jan Bradford; illustrated by Marcy
Ramsey.
    p.   cm.
  Summary: Nine-year-old Caroline receives unexpected help from her
two younger sisters in her plans to earn her own spending money, but
their efforts end up creating a big problem for the entire family.
  ISBN 0-8167-2025-8 (lib. bdg.)   ISBN 0-8167-2026-6 (pbk.)
  [1. Moneymaking projects—Fiction.   2. Sisters—Fiction.]
I. Ramsey, Marcy Dunn, ill.   II. Title.
PZ7.B7228Cat   1991
[Fic]—dc20   90-11156

A TROLL BOOK, published by Troll Associates,
Mahwah, NJ 07430

1

CAROLINE LOVES RODDY

"Quick, Maria! Hit the rewind button!"

When Maria Santiago didn't move fast enough, Caroline Zucker grabbed the VCR's remote control out of her best friend's hand. She couldn't wait another minute to see the concert video of their favorite teen rock star all over again.

Maria didn't object. She said, "It's your turn to rewind the tape anyway. I did it the last three times we watched *Roddy Hastings Live*."

Caroline smiled as the tape whirred inside

the video player. "I love Double Club! I bet the Blue Jays don't do fun things like we do."

At the beginning of the school year, Caroline and Maria had discovered that third-graders weren't allowed to join the Blue Jay Club at Hart Elementary. Instead of getting upset, they had started their own club. It had only two members—Caroline and Maria. Today their meeting was at Maria's house.

"You're right. I heard the Blue Jays are going bird watching this week," Maria told her.

"I'd rather watch Roddy Hastings any day!" Caroline said. "How did you ever convince your mom to rent Roddy's video for our Double Club meeting?"

"I got a hundred percent on my science test yesterday," Maria explained proudly. "When Mom asked what I wanted for a reward, I said Roddy. I guess she couldn't get him in person, so she rented the tape instead."

Caroline giggled at the idea of Mrs. Santiago actually convincing Roddy Hastings to leave California and spend an afternoon with two third-grade girls in Homestead, Colorado.

"Do you think he'll ever do a show in Denver?" Maria asked.

"I don't know." Caroline almost hoped he wouldn't. What if Roddy was that close to her hometown and her parents wouldn't let her go to the concert? "If he did, would your mom let you go?" she asked Maria.

"I couldn't go alone, but I bet she would take me," Maria said.

"Lucky! My mom isn't a Roddy Hastings fan."

"I didn't say my mom *likes* Roddy," Maria pointed out. "I guess our parents are too old to appreciate him."

"That's sad." Caroline was glad she was only nine. "I'd hate to be too old to love Roddy!"

"I love him, too," Maria said. "And remember, I saw him first."

Caroline frowned. "You did not! I saw him on TV *months* ago, and then I told you how great he was!"

"But *I* saw him on the cover of *Rock Times* a week before *you* saw him on TV." Maria frowned, too.

"That doesn't count," Caroline said.

"It does, too."

The video player clicked off, telling them the tape was rewound and ready to be watched for the fourth time. Caroline hit the play button and the girls forgot their argument over who had seen Roddy first. No one was supposed to talk while he was singing—it was a Double Club rule.

Caroline stayed quiet during the first song. But then Roddy Hastings began to sing, "When I met you, girl, it was the first day of my life . . ." and she sighed, "He's so *cute!*"

"You say that every time the tape gets to this part," Maria complained.

Caroline sighed. "I can't help it. Don't you feel as if he's singing this song just for us?"

Maria shook her head. "You must not keep acting like this."

"Why not?" Caroline asked in surprise. Her friend was starting to sound like her mother. Mrs. Zucker thought Caroline spent too much time daydreaming about Roddy Hastings.

"Because it's going to break Michael Hopkins's heart if he finds out how you feel about Roddy," Maria teased.

"Oh, sure." Caroline had had a crush on Michael ever since second grade, but he'd never done anything that made her think he might like her back. "I think you just want to keep me away from Roddy in case he might like me better than you."

Maria laughed so loudly that she almost drowned out the singing. "As if either one of us will ever meet him!"

"You're right," Caroline had to admit. "But it's sure fun to daydream."

Maria leaned close to her and whispered, "I'd love to see the dimple in his chin in person. I want to know if it's real."

"Of course it's real!" Caroline was shocked.

"My mother says there are all kinds of tricks you can do with makeup. Actors and actresses can make dimples or warts or whatever they need to look different." Mrs. Santiago designed costumes for the local theater, and Maria wanted to be an actress when she grew up.

"Makeup!" Caroline refused to believe Roddy Hastings wore makeup. "That's *gross!*"

"Is something wrong, girls?" Maria's mother asked from the archway that opened into the Santiagos' family room.

"No," Maria answered quickly.

"But it sounded like you were arguing."

Caroline couldn't stand to think her favorite singer wasn't all real. "Mrs. Santiago, do you think Roddy is wearing makeup?"

Maria's mother studied the face on the television screen for a minute. "I'm sure he is—all performers do. But if anyone at the Stratford Theater did his makeup, they'd cover that little scar on his cheek . . . and they'd do something to make that cute dimple a little more obvious."

"You like the dimple in his chin?" Caroline asked.

"Don't get all excited," Maria's mother said with a smile. "Just because I think he's kind of cute, doesn't mean I like his music."

"Mom," Maria said in a tone that said she was trying very hard to be patient, "we're *trying* to watch the video, if you don't mind."

"Actually, I wanted to tell you something," Mrs. Santiago told her daughter. "Turn off the tape for just a minute, please."

Maria made a big production of pressing the "pause" button on the remote control. Then she faced her mother. "I'm listening," she sighed.

"Len Hansen was telling me about a class his children took last month—"

Maria explained to Caroline, "Len is one of the actors at the theater where my mom works."

"That's right," Mrs. Santiago said. "His kids had a lot of fun, and they learned a lot in this special class. So I've signed you up for the Saturday afternoon session next month."

Maria narrowed her dark eyes. "What kind of class?"

"Didn't I mention it?" Mrs. Santiago tried to sound surprised. "It's an etiquette class."

"Etiquette?" Maria echoed.

"Yes. A class that teaches children proper manners," her mother explained.

"I know what etiquette means," Maria said. "And I'm not going to go!"

"I've already paid the registration fee." Mrs. Santiago thrust her hands into the pockets of her flowered skirt. Caroline recognized the gesture. Her mother did the same thing, and it meant she did not plan to lose the argument that was just beginning.

Maria must have recognized it, too. She stuck out her chin. "Fine. I'll go—if Caroline goes, too."

"Wait a minute!" Caroline squawked. She had come to Double Club at Maria's house to watch the Roddy Hastings video, not to be signed up for some dumb Saturday afternoon class about manners!

Maria grabbed Caroline's arm. "Please. It won't be so horrible if you come with me."

Mrs. Santiago laughed. "Nothing horrible is going to happen to you, honey."

"I'll just be *bored* to death," Maria grumbled.

"Len's kids said the same thing before the class. But they really had a good time," Mrs. Santiago insisted.

Maria groaned. "But Mom, I already know how to behave. Sit up straight. Don't chew with my mouth open. Always say please and thank you."

"Do you know what to say when someone has been rude to you?" Maria's mother asked, with a twinkle in her eyes.

"I'd say, *Drop dead, creep,*" Maria answered promptly.

"And that would be just as rude. Do you know how to be polite while you make the other person look foolish for having no manners?"

"I'd love it if I could look good while I made Duncan look like a jerk," Caroline said. Duncan Fairbush was in her class at school, and he was always bothering her. "When I try to get back at him for the mean things he does,

7

half the time he turns the trick on me, and I get the blame. It's not fair!"

"Duncan's *never* fair," Maria agreed.

"The class might teach Caroline a few tricks to put Duncan in his place," Mrs. Santiago suggested.

"Maybe." Maria was thoughtful. "Could it teach us how to stop Samantha Collins from acting so snooty all the time?"

"That would be great!" Caroline added. Samantha was only nice to Caroline and Maria when she wanted something. They were used to her being stuck-up, but she'd gotten worse in the past two weeks, ever since her picture won the art contest at the mall.

Maria turned to Caroline. "Wouldn't you just love to be able to show her *politely* that she's not better than us?"

Mrs. Santiago smiled at them both. "I know where you might pick up some pointers."

"I'll go to the class!" Maria cried.

"Don't forget me," Caroline reminded her. "I want to go, too!"

Mrs. Santiago laughed. "Ask your parents about the class tonight," she told Caroline.

The girls clapped their hands and Maria giggled. "We're going to be the politest kids in the whole school!"

Caroline giggled, too. "I can't wait!"

"You won't have to wait to ask your mom about the class," Mrs. Santiago said. "Her car just pulled into the driveway. Time to go home, Caroline."

Caroline glanced at the television screen where Roddy Hastings was frozen, waiting to finish his song.

"But the tape," she said. "We haven't finished watching it."

"I think you've seen it enough times by now to have memorized every second of it," Mrs. Santiago said firmly, picking up Caroline's book bag from a chair.

Caroline stood up slowly. Although she was anxious to tell her mother about the etiquette class, she hated to leave Roddy.

"I promise I won't watch it without you," Maria said.

Mrs. Zucker's car horn honked in the driveway.

"You'd better hurry," Maria told her friend. "Call me tonight when you know if you can take the class!"

2

HELP WANTED

At dinner that night, Mrs. Zucker passed the platter of baked chicken to Caroline and said, "Why don't you tell your father about the etiquette class, honey?"

Across the table, Patricia wrinkled her nose. "Eddy Kett? Who's that?"

Caroline smiled at her seven-year-old sister, feeling very grown-up. Patricia liked to think she knew everything, so it always made Caroline happy to know something she didn't.

"Yeah—who's Eddy Cat?" six-year-old Vicki asked.

"Explain it to Patricia and Vicki," Mrs. Zucker suggested to Caroline. She always wanted the girls to help each other.

"Etiquette means manners," Caroline informed her younger sisters.

"You want to talk to Dad about *manners?*" Patricia was still confused.

Caroline turned to their father. "Mrs. Santiago heard about this etiquette class for kids. Maria is going, and I want to go, too."

Mr. Zucker raised his eyebrows in astonishment. "You do?"

Caroline frowned at him. Did her father think the class was a joke?

"Matt, she's serious," Mrs. Zucker told Mr. Zucker.

Caroline's father took a drink of water. At last he said, "Well, what do you know! I never would have guessed you've been secretly waiting for a chance to polish up your manners."

"*Some* of us don't need to take a *class* to know how to behave," Patricia said with a sniff.

Mrs. Zucker handed the vegetable bowl to Patricia. "And *some* of us haven't had our cauliflower this evening. Help yourself, dear," she said.

Patricia sat tall in her chair, smiled sweetly, and announced, "No thank you, Mother. I don't need any cauliflower tonight."

Their mother smiled. "I fear I must disagree

with you, Miss Patricia. If you want to grow up to be a healthy young lady, you *do* need to eat your vegetables." She scooped a spoonful of cauliflower onto Patricia's plate, and Vicki giggled as Patricia made a face.

Caroline said to her father, "Dad? Can I go to the etiquette class? Mrs. Santiago needs to know so she can reserve a place for me."

Before he could answer, Vicki put in, "I'm learning manners at kindergarten."

"Good for you," Mr. Zucker said solemnly. "You can never start too young. What have you learned so far?"

"Things like not cutting in front of Trevor when it's time to go outside," Vicki replied, "or else he'll break my face."

"That's an important thing to learn," Caroline told her youngest sister, trying not to laugh.

"Will you learn stuff like that at your manners class?" Vicki asked Caroline.

Caroline grinned. "Not exactly. But I'm going to learn how to look good while I make Duncan Fairbush look like a jerk."

Her father nodded. "Now I get it. I thought you were talking about one of those fancy manners courses where you learn which fork to use. But this class sounds useful. Of course, you may go."

Caroline clapped her hands. "I can't wait to tell Maria!"

Mrs. Zucker pointed to Caroline's plate. *"After* you finish your dinner."

"And after you help me stack the dishwasher," Patricia reminded her.

Caroline crossed her fingers and hoped Maria would be home all night.

"Guess what, Maria? I can go to the etiquette class with you!" Caroline cried into the phone at seven o'clock that night.

"All right!" Maria said. Then she added excitedly, "You won't *believe* what I saw in the window of the record store when I went to the mall with Mom!"

"What?"

"Roddy Hastings's new cassette!"

Caroline squealed in delight. "I thought it wasn't due in until next Monday."

"I know." Maria sighed. "But when Mom and I passed Record Whirl, there it was!"

"I've got to go to the mall," Caroline said, frantically trying to think of a way to convince one of her parents to take her there. It wasn't going to be easy—they liked to relax on Friday night.

"Why don't you go talk to your mom?" Maria suggested.

Caroline hung up the phone and raced upstairs to her room under the eaves. Baxter, the Zuckers' half-sheepdog, half-something-else mutt, nearly tripped over his big, shaggy feet as he followed her.

"Close your eyes," she told the dog as she opened her closet door and pulled out her sleeping bag. She kneeled on the floor and unrolled it until she found her money box. It was a square blue box Grandpa Zucker had given her.

Caroline knew she didn't really need to hide her money. No one would ever try to take it, or even borrow it without asking. But she liked to think her money was safe from everyone and everything—even the dream monsters that sometimes sneaked into her room in the middle of the night.

There wasn't a sound as she picked up the box. It usually jingled with dimes and quarters, so the silence wasn't a good sign. Caroline flipped open the clasp and lifted the lid. She couldn't believe what she saw. The box was empty! Caroline turned the box upside down and shook it, but nothing fell out.

Baxter trotted over to the sleeping bag and began sniffing the box.

"Don't waste your time," Caroline told the dog sadly. "I completely forgot that I spent all my money." She sat back on her heels. "Now how am I going to buy the new Roddy Hastings tape?"

Baxter rested his chin on her shoulder as if

he felt sorry for her. Caroline pretended he was talking to her, and she answered him.

"I know it's Friday night, allowance night. But I got mine early this week when Mom and I were shopping Monday night."

Why, oh why, had she spent all the money she'd saved *plus* her allowance on the stuffed penguin and the Little Miss Makeup kit? The penguin was great—Caroline took him to bed with her every night. But the makeup had been a waste of money. The lipstick was invisible when she put it on her lips, and the "perfume" was just a bottle of pink-colored water.

"I'll have to wait *two whole weeks* to save up enough money for that tape," she moaned.

Caroline knew that she could probably borrow Maria's Roddy Hastings tape once or twice, since they were best friends. But it wouldn't be the same. She wouldn't be able to listen to Roddy singing to her while she dressed for school each morning, or when she got ready for bed each night.

"I need my own tape. And I just *can't* wait!"

Leaving the sleeping bag in a heap on her bedroom floor, Caroline raced downstairs, yelling, *"Mommmm—"*

She found her parents in the family room. When she raced through the doorway, her mother looked up from the novel she was reading. Her father had been napping, and he opened one eye.

"What's on your mind?" her mother asked calmly.

Caroline sat on the edge of the rocking chair. "I've got a problem," she said. "I'm hoping you guys can help me."

"Is your math homework causing trouble again?" Mr. Zucker asked.

Caroline shook her head. "This is *much* worse."

Her mother glanced at her father. "It sounds like Caroline has another social studies test on Monday."

Before they could make any more wrong guesses, Caroline told them, "My problem has nothing to do with school. It's personal."

Mrs. Zucker set her novel on the end table. "What can I do to help you, honey?"

Caroline decided it was best to get right to the point. "I need money."

"How much money?" her mother asked.

Caroline crossed her fingers. "Just enough to buy the new Roddy Hastings tape."

"Don't you have all his tapes?"

"Maria went to the mall tonight and found his *new* one. It went on sale today!" Caroline could just see herself walking out of Record Whirl with her very own tape. "I have to get one right away!"

"You want to go to the mall now?" her mother asked in surprise.

"Well, yeah, but I guess tomorrow morning

17

would be okay," Caroline said. "The thing is, I *can't* wait two or three weeks. Will you lend me the money?"

Mrs. Zucker thought about it for a moment. Then she said, "If the tapes just arrived, I imagine the store must have plenty of them. It's unlikely they'll sell them all right away."

Caroline's heart took a dive. She felt as if it was sinking towards her stomach.

"Besides," Mrs. Zucker went on, "you've been getting advances on your allowance almost every week lately. I'm afraid you haven't learned to handle money yet."

"I'll do better next month, honest," Caroline promised. "But Mom, I need the tape *now!*"

"I think you'll be able to survive for a few weeks without it," Mr. Zucker said. His eyes were closed, but his voice was firm. "And if you wait even longer, there will probably be a tape sale at Captain's Discount Outlet. Then you can buy two for the price of one."

The thought of waiting so long, even for *two* Roddy Hastings tapes, was more than Caroline could stand. She had to think of another way to solve her problem.

"Uh . . . Mom and Dad," she said at last, "is there maybe some work I could do around the house to earn some extra money?"

Her father's eyes opened. "I can think of a few projects that need to be done."

"Me, too." Mrs. Zucker stood up. "I'll get some paper so we can make a list."

"A list?" Caroline suddenly realized that her parents might have enough work to keep her busy for years.

"Don't worry, honey," her mother told her. "After we make the list, you can choose which jobs you want to do. This is a very responsible solution to your problem. Good thinking, Caroline!"

3

CAN WEEDS TALK?

"What are you doing after school today?" Maria asked Caroline before class began on Tuesday morning.

"I'm busy," she mumbled.

Maria didn't seem to notice Caroline's answer. She just kept on talking. "My mom is picking me up from school, and she said you can come home with me. We can play my new Roddy Hastings tape on the big stereo in the living room."

Caroline stared at the classroom floor. There was nothing she would rather do than listen to

Roddy singing through the giant speakers connected to the Santiagos' stereo system, but it was impossible.

"I can't go to your house today," Caroline said, finally looking at her friend. "I have work to do at home."

Maria shrugged. Caroline had told her all about her plan to earn money. "Okay. We can do it another time."

Caroline felt an elbow in her ribs just before Duncan Fairbush said, "You're grounded, right, Zucker?"

She decided to try being polite even though she and Maria had not been to their etiquette class yet. She blinked at Duncan. "Excuse me?"

"You're just *pretending* you're busy," he said with a nasty grin on his face. "You don't have to lie. I bet your parents caught you feeding frog legs to your stupid dog, and now you're grounded!"

"I am not!" Caroline yelled. Duncan Fairbush could make her mad faster than anyone in the whole world.

"Then why can't you go to Maria's house?" he asked, narrowing his beady blue eyes.

"I have work to do at home," Caroline answered, determined to keep being polite even if it killed her.

"I don't have to do any work at *my* house," Duncan bragged. "My mom does it all."

Maria decided to stick up for her friend.

"Caroline is working to earn money to buy something she wants. She's being *responsible.*"

"*Oooooh.*" Duncan pretended he was going to faint. "I'm real *impressed,* Zucker!"

"You really have to work today?" Samantha Collins asked. It seemed to Caroline that everybody in the room was eavesdropping on her conversation. "That's too bad," Samantha went on, smoothing her long blond hair. "When I want something, my dad just gives it to me."

When Samantha went to her desk, Maria whispered to Caroline, "I bet her dad *does* give her everything . . . including the award for the best picture in the art contest."

"You know it," Caroline agreed. They had talked about it many times. Student artwork from Hart Elementary had been displayed at the mall, and Samantha's painting of a rainbow had taken first place.

Neither Maria nor Caroline had expected to win. But they both believed there had been a lot of pictures better than Samantha's. The only explanation was that her father owned the We-Love-Toys store at the mall, and the store had sponsored the contest.

Maria grumbled, "I wish I knew what to say to Samantha when she acts so stuck-up."

"We'll both find out next month," Caroline told her friend.

"The etiquette class," Maria whispered, as if it were their secret weapon. "It's too bad we

22

can't tell Samantha about it. It would be nice if *she* learned some manners!"

Caroline giggled.

Their teacher, Mrs. Nicks, clapped her hands at the front of the room. "Good morning, class. Please go to your desks so I can take attendance."

Caroline and Maria hurried to their seats. As Caroline sat down behind Duncan, she made a face at the back of his head. At her desk across the aisle from Duncan, Maria winked at Caroline.

"What are you doing, Santiago?" Duncan yelled. "Are you winking at *me?*"

Caroline had to cover her mouth with both hands to keep from laughing out loud.

"Duncan Fairbush!" Mrs. Nicks snapped. "I'm sure no one was winking at you. Settle down or else I'll have to send you to Principal Fletcher's office again."

"But Mrs. Nicks, she—" Duncan began.

Mrs. Nicks stared at him and he closed his mouth. Caroline loved the way Maria had made Duncan look dumb . . . and she hadn't even been to the etiquette class yet!

"Watch out!" Patricia called just as a basketball whizzed past Caroline's head.

Caroline told herself not to get mad at her sisters. It wasn't their fault that she had agreed to spend the afternoon pulling weeds from among the rocks that surrounded the Zuckers' house. All the houses on their block had rocks around them. But only the Zuckers' rocks were decorated with green weeds.

Caroline caught the ball and tossed it back to Patricia in the driveway. Kneeling on her mother's gardening mat, she watched her sisters for a minute. Neither one of them was tall enough to get the ball into the basket high over their heads.

"Back to the weeds," she told herself with a sigh. Her next victim would be the long, skinny vine snaking across the rocks. Starting at one end, she tried to follow the stem back to the root.

"Where do you belong?" she asked the plant.

A small voice answered, "In the rocks . . ." and Caroline jumped in surprise.

Patricia and Vicki began to laugh behind her. Caroline turned to look up at them, using her hand to shade her eyes from the afternoon sun.

"Did you really think the weed was talking to you?" Vicki asked between giggles.

"Of course not. I just didn't expect anyone to be sneaking up on me, that's all," Caroline said. It was bad enough that they'd caught her talking to a plant. She certainly wasn't going to admit that for just one part of a second, she had wondered if the weed *was* talking to her.

24

"Can you play with us for a little while?" Vicki asked.

"We want to play Keep-Away," Patricia explained. "But it's hard to play it without a third person."

"Yeah." Vicki nodded her curly head. "We don't have anyone to stand in the middle, so there's nobody to keep the ball away from."

Caroline sighed. "That's too bad, guys. But I've got to finish this project today."

"You're no fun," Patricia told her, pouting.

"Then let's go inside and play a video game," Vicki said.

Caroline watched as the girls headed toward the back door. She wished she could have played with them, but this job was more important. When her parents paid her, she would have almost enough money to buy the tape. Only one project was left—sorting her mother's stack of grocery coupons and throwing away any that had expired. Caroline planned to do that the next night while she watched some good shows on television.

For a minute she thought about the kids at school. Duncan said his mother did everything for him, and Samantha was proud that her father gave her anything she wanted. It was strange, but Caroline actually felt good about working so hard to earn the money for her Roddy Hastings tape. When she listened to Roddy's new songs, they would belong to only

25

her. And no one would be able to take them away from her, because she had *earned* them. She went back to the "talking" weed, humming one of her favorite Roddy Hastings songs while she worked.

4

MUSIC, MUSIC, MUSIC

"Thank you, Daddy," Vicki said with a smile on Friday evening as Mr. Zucker handed out the girls' allowances.

When Patricia got hers, she carefully counted the three one-dollar bills. Then she thanked her father.

Caroline's fingers were itching as she waited for her allowance. The money she'd earned working for her parents was in her jeans pocket. When Mr. Zucker handed Caroline her allowance, she threw her arms around his neck. "Thanks, Dad!"

She ran into the kitchen. "Mom? Could we go to the mall now?"

"It must be allowance time," Mrs. Zucker said. She was rinsing out the thermos she always took to the hospital where she worked as a nurse.

The thermos reminded Caroline that her mother had had a busy day. Although she didn't know how she could possibly wait until the next morning to buy her cassette tape, she said quickly, "I'll understand if you're too tired."

Mrs. Zucker smiled. "Why, thank you, Caroline—that was very thoughtful. But there are a few things I want to buy at the mall, too."

"Hooray!" Caroline shouted. "Thanks, Mom!"

Mrs. Zucker hugged her. Then she said, "Well, don't just stand there—get my purse and we'll sneak out of here."

But when Vicki saw Caroline carrying their mother's shoulder bag, she followed her sister into the kitchen. "Are we going somewhere, Mom?" she asked.

"I'm going out with Caroline for a while, honey," Mrs. Zucker said.

"Where?" Patricia asked, coming into the kitchen, too.

"We have some shopping to do," Mrs. Zucker explained.

"I need new piano music," Patricia announced and waved her allowance money in the air. "I can pay for it myself."

"Maybe we can do that tomorrow." Mrs. Zucker took her purse from Caroline and searched for her car keys.

Patricia folded her arms across her chest and shouted, "Not fair!"

Vicki copied Patricia's actions. "Not fair to little kids!"

"Hey, *I'm* not a little kid," Patricia cried.

"You're more little than Mom or Caroline," Vicki pointed out.

"You should take all of us shopping."

Just in case her mother was starting to change her mind, Caroline tugged on her sleeve. "Mom, let's go."

Mrs. Zucker nodded. "If we don't leave soon, the mall will close for the night before we have a chance to do our shopping. Patricia and Vicki, take good care of your father and Baxter while we're gone."

Caroline skipped out the back door behind her mother. "Thanks again, Mom," she said. "I really didn't want them to come with us."

Mrs. Zucker patted Caroline's shoulder. "I know. Tonight's shopping trip is for *big* girls only!"

Several hours later, Caroline's father stuck his head into her room. "Hi, honey," he said, but Caroline didn't see or hear him. She was

29

lying on her bed listening to the new tape with her eyes shut tight. It was every bit as wonderful as she'd thought it would be.

"I said, HI, HONEY," Mr. Zucker yelled. This time Caroline heard him. She opened her eyes, turned off the pocket-sized cassette player, and took the earplugs out of her ears.

"I hope you don't mind that I'm using your Porta-Tunes," she said. "Mom said I could."

"It's perfectly all right." He leaned against the door frame. "Is the tape good?"

Caroline smiled so broadly that her face ached. "It's absolutely fantastic!"

"It's been a long time since I've been excited about a new album," her father told her.

Caroline offered the earplugs to him. "Want to listen?"

He chuckled. "No thanks. I just came up here to ask if you're ever going to go to bed tonight."

Talking about bed made Caroline suddenly feel tired. She stifled a yawn. "Let me listen to the tape just one more time."

Her father smiled. "And one time after that, and one time after that, and . . ."

Caroline felt her cheeks growing hot.

"Enjoy yourself," Mr. Zucker said. "I bet you'll fall asleep listening to it." He blew her a kiss. "Good night, Caroline. Sweet dreams."

" 'Night, Dad. Tell Mom, too." Before he closed the door, she threw him two kisses, one for him and one for her mother.

Caroline waited until her father went down-stairs to put the earplugs in again. She was just in time to hear Roddy's slow song about moving to a new town and missing all his old friends.

The gentle rhythm of the music began to make Caroline feel sleepy. Her eyelids started to close, and her head felt suddenly heavy.

"I'll just get more comfortable," she said to her goldfish, even though she knew Justin and Esmerelda were probably sleeping. It was hard to tell when they were really asleep because they didn't close their eyes. But they weren't swimming or even waving their fins—they were just floating in one place, looking bored.

Caroline fluffed up her pillow and rested her head on it. Lying on her back, she could look at the sparkling stars on the slanted ceiling over her head. Her father had used glitter paint to make the stars after Caroline and her sisters had painted the room four different colors to cover her ugly wallpaper.

Soon Caroline's feet began to feel cold. She crawled under her quilted bedspread. In spite of all her promises, her eyelids slowly closed, and she fell asleep while Roddy kept on singing. . . .

"I'm sorry," Caroline told her father at breakfast the next morning as she handed him the dead Porta-Tunes. "I fell asleep and used up the battery."

"But the tape is all right?" he asked with a grin. Caroline was relieved. She had been afraid he'd be angry and tell her how expensive batteries were, but instead, he was worried about her tape. She smiled back at him. "Roddy's fine."

Roddy Hastings was so fine that Caroline planned to play the tape over and over and over on the stereo in the family room. She might listen to it all day long while she did her special project for English. No one else ever used the stereo much, except when her parents sometimes sat on the couch in the dark and played old records late at night.

Caroline collected all the materials she needed for her project—marker pens, colored paper, glue, scissors and a stack of magazines. Each student in Mrs. Nicks' class had to make up a story and tell it with pictures, and Caroline planned to use the Woofee Pet Food dog as the subject for her story. There were hundreds of Woofee ads in the magazines she'd collected.

There was one more thing in her stack of work materials—the new Roddy Hastings tape. Caroline brought everything into the family room. With a grin, she popped her cassette into the tape player and punched the right buttons.

"Who needs money? Who needs fame? All I need is you," Roddy sang, his voice filling the room.

"All I need is *you!*" Caroline sang along with him. Then she sat cross-legged on the floor next to her pile of magazines, humming and flipping through the glossy pages until she found the Woofee Pet Food dog smiling at her.

The dog looked so real that she barked at him. "Woof!"

Baxter must have thought she was talking to him, because he came tearing into the room and slid to a stop in front of her. Magazines flew in every direction.

But Caroline didn't get mad at him. Scratching Baxter behind the ears, she told him, "I bet you just wanted to listen, too. Smart dog."

He stretched out next to her and closed his eyes. Caroline carefully pulled the magazines from beneath his heavy, shaggy body. Although she planned to get right to work on her project, now it was time for her favorite song on the new tape.

She sang along with Roddy word for word. She clapped her hands when Roddy clapped his. The best part of using her parents' stereo was the automatic reverse. She wouldn't have to get up to flip the tape. On its own, the machine would play the second side. And when the second side was over, the first side would play again. Roddy could sing for hours while she cut out pictures from the magazines.

Her plan was to show the Woofee dog's adventures in one afternoon. He was going to chase a cat up a tree. And then, if she could find the right pictures, he was going to save a little boy who had chased a ball into the street without looking for cars first.

Caroline had no idea how long she had been working when she heard Patricia come into the room. "If I hear that guy singing for another minute, I'm going to be sick!" Patricia said.

"Don't be sick in here. Mom gets upset when people throw up on the carpet," Caroline told her sister without looking up.

"I'm not leaving," Patricia announced. "I have to play my Beethoven tape."

"Now?" Caroline couldn't believe her ears.

"Mrs. Church said I have to listen to it before my next piano lesson."

"Can't you use Dad's Porta—never mind." Caroline knew Patricia couldn't use their father's cassette player until he bought more batteries. She sighed. "Okay."

Patricia smiled at her. "It'll only take an hour."

An *hour* away from Roddy after she had worked so hard to earn the tape? Caroline swallowed hard. "All right. I'll leave my project here and be back in an hour."

35

"But I need to listen to *my* music, too," Vicki said from the doorway.

"What music?" Caroline had no idea what Vicki meant.

"Snuggle Kittens." Vicki held out a cassette case. Caroline read the label: *All your favorite songs from the television cartoon show.*

"I changed my mind." Caroline gathered up her things in such a rush that Baxter woke up. "I'll take my stuff upstairs since I probably won't be able to use the stereo until sometime tomorrow afternoon!"

"It won't take *that* long," Patricia called after her.

Caroline ignored her. She wished with all her heart she hadn't let her father's Porta-Tunes run all night. If the batteries were still good, she could listen to Roddy anywhere at all.

After Caroline took her materials and the tape up to her room, she went looking for her father. Maybe she could talk him into driving to the store for batteries. Instead, she found her mother in the kitchen and asked, "Where's Dad?"

"Jogging with a friend."

Caroline changed her plan. "Mom, could we drive to the drug store?"

"Why?" Her mother used her finger to mark her place in the cookbook she was using. "I don't need anything."

"We need batteries for Dad's Porta-Tunes."

Mrs. Zucker smiled. "That's nice of you to think about your father. But he took it with him. He was going to get some batteries before he started jogging."

Caroline bit her lip. The Porta-Tunes was probably clipped on her father's belt while he ran. She realized that she couldn't use it any time she wanted—it belonged to her father. There was only one solution.

"Mom? I need my own Porta-Tunes," Caroline said.

Mrs. Zucker closed her book. "I'm afraid not."

Caroline frowned. "I'm just asking for one little radio and cassette player."

"It's not just one," Mrs. Zucker said with a sigh. "I can't buy one Porta-Tunes. I'd have to buy *three* of them."

"Why?"

"If you have one, your sisters will each want to have their own," she explained.

"But they don't *need* their own."

"This discussion is finished," her mother said firmly.

Caroline knew better than to argue any longer. When her mother said a discussion was finished, it was finished. Period. Caroline left the kitchen, but she didn't give up.

Since her mother wouldn't buy her a Porta-Tunes, she would ask her father. But then her parents would probably talk it over, and her father would agree with her mother. Grown-ups always stuck together. If she wanted a personal cassette player, she would have to buy it herself.

Caroline found the morning paper and checked every page until she found an advertisement for Porta-Tunes. She gasped as she read the price out loud.

"Forty dollars!"

By the time she saved that much, she would be in sixth grade! She couldn't wait that long. There had to be a way to earn more money, but she couldn't pull weeds and sort coupons every week. She would have to think of a better plan.

5

SUNFLOWERS AND SNAPDRAGONS

On Sunday afternoon, Caroline went to Maria's house. She loved Maria's bedroom with its pale walls and the skylight in the ceiling. But at that moment, she was more interested in the magazine lying open on Maria's rose-colored quilt.

"Aren't you *ever* going to stop staring at that picture?" Maria asked after Caroline had been stretched out on the bed looking at the magazine for a very long time. She could not take her eyes off the full-page color photograph of Roddy Hastings' face.

39

"It's not like I'm going to wear it out or anything," Caroline said.

Maria giggled. "I stared at it for about an hour last night. There are some other pictures of him near the back of the magazine."

Caroline immediately started turning pages, looking for Roddy. Then something even more exciting caught her attention.

It was an ad that read: *Win the prizes you want. Sell flower seeds!* Just below the banner, there was a picture of a Porta-Tunes!

"I *have* to do this!" she cried.

"What?" Maria jumped off her chair so fast that it almost tipped over. "Did I miss a really good picture of Roddy?"

"Look at this!" Caroline folded the magazine open to the Porta-Tunes page and shoved it under Maria's nose.

"It's an ad for selling flower seeds." Maria frowned. "I'm worried about you, Caroline. I think Roddy Hastings is making you crazy."

"Forget the seeds." Caroline pointed at the radio and cassette player. "This is my new Porta-Tunes!"

Maria took the magazine, sat on the edge of the bed, and read the advertisement. Then she said, "You *can't* forget the seeds. If you don't sell them, you won't get the Porta-Tunes."

Caroline grinned. "No problem. It will be a lot easier than saving my allowance for the next hundred years!"

"Maybe . . ." Maria said thoughtfully.

"Can I cut out the form?" Caroline asked.

Maria quickly checked the back of the page to see if there was anything important on it. "Go ahead."

Caroline snipped along the dotted lines. "I'm going to fill this out tonight and have my dad mail it tomorrow," she said excitedly. "I wonder how soon I'll get my Porta-Tunes."

"Not before our etiquette class," Maria guessed.

"Well, I couldn't listen to my tape during the class anyway, could I?"

"No way." Maria sounded very sure of herself. "They'll probably tell you it's rude to walk around with earplugs stuck in your ears."

"What do you think they'll teach us?" Caroline was beginning to get worried. What if she found out that she had the worst manners in the class?

Maria wrinkled her forehead while she thought about Caroline's question. Finally, she said, "I *did* see one thing in an old movie my mom was watching last night."

"What?" Caroline asked.

"You have to stand up," Maria told her.

She took a dictionary from her desk. When Caroline stood next to the bed, Maria set the book on top of her friend's head.

"Ouch! It's heavy!"

"Don't complain," Maria said. "This is impor-

tant. A *real* lady walks so straight that a book won't fall off her head."

"Did you have to use such a *big* book?" Caroline asked. "If it falls off, it could break my foot!" She took one small step and the book slid right off her head.

Maria caught the dictionary before it could hit the floor—or Caroline's foot. She shook her head and sighed. "It looks like we've got a lot of work to do if we want to be ready for that class."

"They're here!" Caroline screamed when she got home from school on Friday afternoon and saw the big box on the kitchen table.

"Who's here?" Patricia asked, coming into the room.

"I hope it's Grandpa Nevelson," Vicki said. "Maybe he brought us candy from his store."

Caroline looked up at them and explained, "It's my seeds! Now I can win my very own Porta-Tunes."

"Lucky duck," Patricia said enviously.

"Want me to help you open the box?" Laurie Morrell asked. Laurie was a high-school student who baby-sat for the Zucker girls when both their parents were at work.

"Oh, yes!" Caroline cried. Laurie helped her open the box.

"This looks like serious work. You'll need this," Laurie said, setting a tall glass of lemonade in front of Caroline. She poured lemonade for Patricia and Vicki, too.

"Thanks," Caroline said. She unfolded a glossy sheet and spread it out on the table. It showed all the different kinds of flower seeds in her packets: marigolds, zinnias, morning glories, sunflowers, and one of her favorites— snapdragons.

"What do you have to do to win the radio?" Laurie asked.

"It's not just a radio. It plays tapes, too." Caroline turned the sheet over. The prize list was at the bottom of the page.

She started to drink her lemonade as she read the list—and began to choke.

"Are you all right?" Laurie asked anxiously.

Caroline coughed a few times and gasped. Once she caught her breath, she said, "I'll *never* be all right! I have to sell *two hundred and fifty* seed packets to get the Porta-Tunes!"

"Wow!" said Patricia.

Laurie whistled. "That's a lot."

Vicki raced out of the kitchen. A moment later she came back with a handful of nickels and dimes. "I'll buy a pack of seeds," she said.

Patricia added, "I want to buy a pack, too."

"Thanks, guys." Caroline thought her sisters were being very sweet. Now she only had to sell two hundred and forty-eight packets!

* * *

"Are you sure you want to buy ten packs of seeds?" Caroline asked her Grandpa Nevelson later that evening after the whole family had finished supper.

"Of course I do," he answered.

"But you don't have a garden," she reminded him.

His eyes twinkled as he said, "Who needs a garden? I'm buying them because I like the pictures on the packets!"

Before she gave the seeds to her grandfather, she hugged him. "Thank you, Grandpa."

He patted her head and kissed her cheek. "Always happy to help my favorite girls."

Vicki wriggled between Caroline and Grandpa Nevelson. "If I was selling seeds, would you buy some from me?"

He nodded his white head. "I'm sure I'll be buying seeds and cookies and candy bars from all three of you for many years to come."

"The fifth-graders at our school are selling pizzas to raise money for their field trip," Patricia told him.

Their grandpa pressed a hand to his stomach and groaned. "I hope I won't have to buy pizzas when each of you is in fifth grade."

"How can you hate pizza?" Caroline asked him. It was the only thing about her grandfather that made it hard for her to believe they were related.

"I tried it once and those dead fish made me

sick," he explained as he always did when they talked about pizza.

"But Grandpa," Patricia said in her I-know-everything voice, "you don't *have* to get anchovies on your pizza."

He just shook his head. Caroline knew that no one was ever going to convince him there was any other kind of pizza.

Caroline punched him in the arm. "We love you anyway, Grandpa Nevelson."

He grinned at all three of his granddaughters. "I love all of you, too."

By the time Grandpa Nevelson went home, it was time for bed. Caroline slowly climbed the steps to her bedroom. Her brain was spinning as she tried to figure out how long it would take before she could get her Porta-Tunes.

Patricia, Vicki, and Grandpa Nevelson were not the only people who had bought seeds from her that day. Laurie had taken two packs, and when Caroline phoned Maria to tell her the seed order had arrived, Mrs. Santiago had ordered five packets. Her parents had bought seven packs. She was so glad she had found the advertisement in Maria's magazine. It must have been her lucky day.

6

SELLING SEEDS ISN'T EASY

On Monday, Caroline and Maria stayed in the classroom when it was time for recess.

"Aren't you girls going outside today?" Mrs. Nicks asked.

Maria nudged Caroline with her elbow and whispered, "Ask her."

"Uh—Mrs. Nicks?" Caroline's mouth got very dry. She swallowed hard.

"Yes, Caroline? Do you have a problem?"

"No problem. I was just wondering if you would like to buy some flower seeds," she said quickly. "I'm trying to win a prize."

"Flower seeds?" Mrs. Nicks sounded interested. "What kind do you have?"

Caroline tried to open the large, glossy sheet with all the flower pictures, but the paper would not unfold. Maria had to help—it took two pairs of hands.

Mrs. Nicks laid the page on her desk and studied it. "Hmmm . . ."

After a few minutes, Mrs. Nicks folded the sheet and gave it back to Caroline. To her delight, the teacher said, "I'd like two packets of marigold seeds, two zinnias, and one pack of snapdragons."

"You would?" Caroline squeaked. "I mean, I'll bring them to school for you tomorrow!"

"And I'll bring the money," Mrs. Nicks said with a smile. "Now run along and play."

Maria and Caroline raced to the playground, giggling. "I can't believe it!" Maria said. "No-Nonsense Nicks is actually buying five packs of seeds from you!"

Caroline beamed. "Now I only have to sell two hundred and nineteen more packs."

Maria said, "I bet you'll have them all sold by the weekend."

"I hope my Porta-Tunes comes right away after I send in the money," Caroline said happily.

"Wouldn't it be great if we could both bring our cassette players and our Roddy Hastings tapes to our next Double Club meeting?"

Maria's eyes sparkled with excitement. "We could listen to our tapes and dance without anyone else hearing our music. We wouldn't have to stay at my house—we could dance anywhere!"

"I can't wait!" Caroline imagined them dancing down the sidewalk to the park by Maria's house. People would probably think they were crazy, but they were going to have so much fun!

The minute school was over that afternoon, Caroline started going from house to house on her block. Her first stop was Mrs. Simpson's.

"Be sure to smile," Patricia reminded her as Caroline rang the bell.

"But old Mrs. Simpson is so *mean*," Vicki said, hiding behind Patricia.

The door opened a crack and Caroline put a big smile on her face. "Good afternoon, Mrs. Simpson."

The door opened wider. Mrs. Simpson was very tall, so she had to look down—and then farther down—before she saw the Zucker girls. "Yes?" she said.

Caroline opened her glossy sheet full of pictures of flowers. She had been practicing so she could do it by herself. "I'm selling seeds. I have seeds for snapdragons, sunflowers, morning glories—"

Mrs. Simpson held up her hand like a policeman stopping traffic. "You're too late, Caroline. I planted my garden two weeks ago. Isn't your garden planted already?"

She shook her head. Caroline's family never planted their garden until the last weekend of school. It was her father's way for all of them to celebrate the beginning of summer vacation.

Mrs. Simpson began closing her door. "Sorry."

"I don't think she *sounded* very sorry," Patricia said as they walked to the next house.

The Hawkes' house was next. They had five children, all of them older than Caroline. She rang the doorbell and hoped Mrs. Hawke would be the one to answer it. But fifteen-year-old Sammy opened the door instead.

Caroline lifted her sales sheet with the flower pictures. "I'm selling seeds."

"Yeah?" He pushed his long hair out of his eyes and squinted at her display sheet. "What kind of seeds?"

"Zinnias, snapdragons . . ." Caroline got quiet when Sammy wrinkled his nose.

"Any carrots or cucumbers?" he asked.

Caroline shook her head. "Only flowers."

Sammy shrugged. Then he said, "You can't eat flowers. We just grow vegetables."

"Thanks," Caroline sighed and hurried down the steps.

The girls stopped at each house on their

block. Most of the people had finished planting their gardens. One other family grew only vegetables. Finally, there were just two houses left: Mrs. Heppler's and Mr. Grumbel's.

"Not Mr. Grumbel!" Vicki cried when Caroline started up the path to his door.

"He won't buy anything," Patricia said. Caroline didn't blame her sisters for wanting to skip the red house with the heavy curtains at the windows. Mr. Grumbel was a scary old man. Even his name wasn't friendly!

"I've got to sell these seeds to someone," Caroline told her sisters. "I'm going to ask him. But you can wait here."

She pressed the button and listened as the doorbell echoed inside the house. Next, she heard slow footsteps. At last, the door opened.

Caroline thought Mr. Grumbel was probably as old as Grandpa Nevelson. He had white hair like her grandfather, but that was the only thing they had in common. Grandpa Nevelson was tall and handsome; Mr. Grumbel was a short man with beady eyes. And those dark bird-eyes were staring at Caroline through Mr. Grumbel's screen door.

She coughed to clear away the tightness in her throat. "Hi, Mr. Grumbel. I'm Caroline Zucker. I live over there." She pointed across Hawthorne Street.

"Zucker . . ." He thought for a minute or two.

Rubbing his chin, he said, "What do you want?"

"Oh . . ." Caroline held her seed sheet up to the screen. "I'm selling flower seeds."

He opened the screen door a crack and reached for the glossy paper. "Could I see that?"

She let him take it inside, hoping he would give it back when he was done looking at it.

Mr. Grumbel read the descriptions under each picture very carefully. He peered at one kind of flower, and then another.

Caroline held her breath. Was he actually going to buy some seeds? She counted the number of times his finger moved from one picture to the next. According to her count, he might buy four seed packets. She was smiling when he finally looked up from the paper.

He pointed to the sunflowers. "I would like these."

"And?"

"Just the sunflowers," he told her.

"How many packets?" Caroline asked hopefully.

"One."

"Great." Caroline tried not to sound as disappointed as she felt. She slipped her backpack off her shoulders and took out one small package.

He opened the door just wide enough for them to make a trade. Caroline handed him the sunflower seeds. He returned the picture sheet and gave her money for the packet.

"Thank you," Caroline said as she put the backpack on again.

"These will grow very tall," he told her.

"I know." Caroline didn't want to stand on Mr. Grumbel's front step all afternoon, but she didn't want to be rude, either. "We grew sunflowers last year in our backyard."

"If you'd like, you can come over and see mine. They should be blooming in late July."

"I'll think about it," she told him and went back down the path. Talking with Mr. Grumbel hadn't been hard at all, but she didn't really want to come back to visit his sunflowers.

"Let's go to Mrs. Heppler's house," Vicki said when Caroline joined her and Patricia. "I bet she'll give us cookies."

"Wait a minute," Patricia said. She turned to Caroline. "I can't *believe* Grumpy Grumbel bought seeds from you. What did he get?"

"One pack of sunflower seeds," she said as Vicki grabbed her hand and started pulling her toward Mrs. Heppler's white house.

"Just one?" Patricia walked next to her sisters. "Why did it take so long for him to buy one pack?"

"We were talking. He invited me back to see the flowers this summer."

Patricia's mouth fell open. "He asked you to

come back to his house? Are you going to do it?"

"I don't know," Caroline said slowly. "Mr. Grumbel isn't really scary. I think he's just lonely."

"Of course he's lonely," Patricia said as they walked up the Hepplers' driveway. "No one ever goes to his house."

"Because everybody's scared of him," Vicki added. "Don't go back, Caroline."

"I might," Caroline said. Mr. Grumbel might not be so bad after all.

Mrs. Heppler opened her door before the girls reached her step. "Good afternoon, Caroline, Patricia and Vicki. What can I do for you today?" she asked, smiling.

"Caroline is selling flower seeds," Patricia told her.

"Hmm . . ." Mrs. Heppler tapped her fingers against the door frame. "I've already planted my garden."

"Can't you buy *something?*" Vicki asked. "Nobody wants her seeds."

Caroline felt her face turning red. It was nice that her sisters were trying to help her, but she was embarrassed.

"Show me what you have," Mrs. Heppler said to Caroline. "I bet I can find something I'd like to buy. Why don't you all come inside?"

While she looked over the flower pictures, the girls ate cookies. Little Billy Heppler tried to stuff three cookies into his mouth at once. It made an awful mess.

"I love snapdragons," Mrs. Heppler said at last.

Caroline grinned. "So do I. They're my favorites."

"Could I get one pack?"

"Sure," Caroline said politely in spite of her disappointment. In an hour, she had sold only two packs of seeds. Where was she ever going to find enough people to buy the two hundred and seventeen packets still in her backpack?

"I'll never get my Porta-Tunes," she told her sisters as they trudged home from Mrs. Heppler's house.

"Maybe we can help," Patricia said, putting her arm around Caroline's waist.

Caroline sighed. "How?"

Vicki squeezed her hand. "Don't worry. We'll think of something!"

7

THE BIG SECRET

The next morning, Maria was waiting for Caroline outside Hart Elementary. As they walked into school together, Maria asked, "Anything interesting happen at your house last night?"

"Nothing special." Caroline had been tired and upset about her bad luck with the flower seeds, so she had finished her homework, watched a little television, and gone to bed early.

Maria twisted a handful of her long, dark hair into a rope as they reached their classroom. "I didn't understand our math homework. It took me almost an hour to find someone who could help me."

Caroline was confused. "Why didn't you call? I could have explained it to you."

"I *tried* to call you. I tried *five times,*" Maria said.

"I forgot about my sisters!" Caroline slapped herself on the forehead.

Duncan Fairbush walked into the room just in time to see that. He laughed and yelled, "Hit yourself again, Zucker! Maybe it will make your brain work better!"

"What about your sisters?" Maria asked, ignoring Duncan.

Caroline ignored him, too. Turning her back on Duncan, she told her friend, "They were totally weird last night."

"Did Patricia glue herself to the piano bench?" Maria asked with a giggle.

Caroline laughed, too. Patricia loved practicing the piano so she would do well at her weekly lesson. "I bet she'd do anything to get compliments from her piano teacher."

"Did Patricia have a lesson last night?" Maria asked.

"No." Caroline shook her head. "She and Vicki took turns making phone calls last night."

"All night?"

"Just about. I never knew they had so many friends," Caroline said. "And when they weren't talking on the telephone, they were hiding in their room."

"It sounds like they have a big secret," Maria guessed. "What do you think they're planning?"

Caroline used her finger to draw a big question mark in the air. "Who knows? Little sisters are impossible to understand. Sometimes I think you're lucky to be an only child!"

"What's going on here?" Maria asked Caroline later that day. They were standing in the lunch line, and everyone at the front of the line was whispering to each other.

As they got closer to the food, the girls heard more whispering. Caroline tipped her head to listen carefully. "I don't think they're talking about lunch. It's something about winning a prize."

"There's a contest?" Maria smiled. "I love winning things!"

"Me, too. Like a Porta-Tunes," Caroline added.

She and Maria didn't see the sign until their class reached the head of the line.

"Look!" Maria pointed to the poster taped to the wall.

In uneven hand-printed letters, it said: WIN A $100 SHOPPING SPREE AT WE-LOVE-TOYS! MEET AT THE BIKE RACK AFTER SCHOOL.

"A hundred dollars of free stuff from We-Love-Toys?" Caroline asked.

"Samantha's dad owns that store," Maria said.

But Caroline didn't care about Samantha for once. "There's so much great stuff at We-Love-Toys. It doesn't matter who the store belongs to. Are you going to go to the bike rack?"

Maria frowned. "My mom expects me home right after school. Will you find out what we have to do to win? I'll call you tonight."

"It's a deal." Caroline could hardly wait to learn the rules of the contest.

Caroline planned to race to the bike rack the minute classes were over, but Mrs. Nicks wanted to talk to her about next month's science fair. She promised the teacher she would discuss a project with Maria. Then she hurried into the hall, heading for the school's back door.

"Hey, Zucker!"

Caroline didn't even turn around to see who it was. She would know Duncan Fairbush's voice anywhere.

"Slow down," he called. "You're walking so fast that your hair is sticking out all over. It looks like the mop in my mom's kitchen closet."

Caroline kept on walking.

"Are you going to the bike rack?" Duncan asked.

If she didn't answer him, she knew he'd just keep asking more questions, so Caroline said, "Yes. I want to know about the contest."

"Don't bother," he said, catching up with her. "Because *I'm* going to win the hundred dollars' worth of toys!"

Caroline raised her eyebrows. "Oh, yeah?"

"Yeah!" As they went out the back door, they passed Samantha Collins. She glared at Caroline.

"What's her problem?" Duncan asked.

"She probably can't believe I'm walking with you. I can't believe it either." Caroline started to walk faster.

"You're not going to find out about the prize before me," he yelled, catching up with her again.

They raced down the hill and pushed their way through the crowd around the bike rack. Of course, when they got close, Duncan shoved Caroline out of his way.

When Caroline finally saw what was going on, she was astonished. Patricia and Vicki were taking money from people and handing them something in return. What on earth were her sisters doing?

Now she was close enough to hear Patricia's voice. Her sister was saying, "Just two dollars for a pack of flower seeds *and* a chance to win the prize!"

Flower seeds? Caroline couldn't believe they were selling *her* seeds, but what other seeds could they have? She decided to wait for her turn to enter the contest.

"Two dollars, please," Patricia said without looking up when Caroline stepped forward. She handed scraps of paper and stubby pencils to Caroline and three other kids.

"What do I do with this?" a boy next to Caroline asked.

"Write your name on it and we'll put it into the box for the drawing. A week from Saturday, one name will be picked." While she talked, Patricia collected papers and money from the kids who had finished writing their names. She gave each of them a packet of seeds from Caroline's kit.

Vicki saw Caroline first. She pulled on Patricia's sleeve. When Patricia just kept handing out paper and seeds, Vicki pulled harder.

"Stop it!" Patricia told her. "You'll make me drop these."

"But it's *Caroline!*"

Patricia raised her head and found herself staring straight at Caroline. She swallowed hard and said, "Uh—hi."

Caroline leaned over the bike rack and hissed, "What are you *doing*?"

Vicki smiled. "Helping you."

Caroline blinked. *"Helping* me? You have to stop this!"

Patricia reached around Caroline to hand out more slips of paper. Then she told her sister, "We can't stop until we take care of all these people."

Caroline realized that Patricia was right. If she said no one else could enter the contest, the kids would probably start a riot.

"I'll talk to you both later," she told her sisters. Then Caroline squeezed out of the crowd and sat down under some aspen trees near the playground.

Half an hour later, Patricia and Vicki walked over to her.

"We're done," Patricia said cheerfully.

"We sure got a lot of names," Vicki said. She showed Caroline a box full of little square pieces of paper.

Caroline grabbed the box. "What do you guys think you're doing?" she squawked.

Patricia unzipped her backpack and showed Caroline all the dollar bills she had collected. "Selling your flower seeds," she said proudly.

"But who's going to pay a hundred dollars to the toy store for the shopping spree?" Caroline asked.

"What do you mean?" Vicki sounded very puzzled.

"Stores give away shopping sprees all the

time. And radio stations give away prizes every day," Patricia explained with confidence.

"But someone has to pay for the prizes in those contests," Caroline told her sisters. How could they be so silly?

"You mean *we* have to pay We-Love-Toys?" Vicki began to chew her bottom lip the way she always did when she was about to cry.

Caroline put her arms around her youngest sister. "Don't cry, Vicki. I'll think of something."

"What?" Patricia asked. Her blue eyes were full of worry. "We'll never get a hundred dollars in less than two weeks unless we use the money we just collected. And if we do that, you won't get your Porta-Tunes. We might as well need a *million* dollars." Patricia sank to the ground in a heap. "We were only trying to help you. . . ."

"Yeah," Vicki said. "We sold all your seed packs."

"*All* of them?" Caroline felt a huge lump in her throat, and her eyes filled with tears. Since her sisters had done so much for her, she *had* to figure out a way to solve their problem.

"Maybe you could get Samantha to help," Patricia suggested.

Caroline stared at her. "Samantha Collins?"

"Doesn't her father own We-Love-Toys?"

"He sure does. But Samantha doesn't like me," Caroline said. Suddenly she remembered how Samantha had glared at her when she and Duncan were leaving the school. Now she knew why Samantha had looked so angry. There was no way that Samantha would help the Zucker girls out of this mess.

Vicki started chewing her lower lip again. "Mom and Daddy are going to be real mad when they find out," she said in a wobbly voice.

Caroline forced a smile. "We'll just have to hope they don't find out right away. Don't cry, Vicki. I said I'd think of something, and I will. I promise."

8

UH, OH!

But though Caroline thought until her head felt as if it would explode, she couldn't come up with a single plan. All three girls were very quiet at supper that evening. As soon as they had finished their chores, Patricia and Vicki scurried to their bedroom. Caroline was about to go upstairs to her own room when the doorbell rang. She paused on the steps to see who the visitor was. When her father opened the door, Caroline gasped. It was Mr. Collins, Samantha's father.

Now her sisters were in deep trouble. Caroline needed more time to think of a plan to help them, but time had just run out.

"Mr. Zucker?" said Mr. Collins.

"Yes, I'm Matt Zucker," her father replied.

"I'm Steve Collins. I think we need to talk," Mr. Collins said.

Looking puzzled, Caroline's father said, "We do? Won't you come in, Mr. Collins?" He led the way into the living room and introduced Mr. Collins to Caroline's mother. Then he offered Mr. Collins a chair, but Mr. Collins didn't sit down.

He didn't waste any time in coming to the point. "What can you tell me about the shopping spree at We-Love-Toys?"

"Excuse me?" Mr. Zucker frowned.

Caroline knew she should have explained the situation to her parents, but it was too late now. She wanted to run and hide, but instead she crept down the stairs and peeked into the living room.

"It seems your girls have been selling chances after school for a hundred-dollar shopping spree at *my* toy store," Mr. Collins was saying.

"*Our* girls?" Mrs. Zucker said faintly.

"Are you sure?" Mr. Zucker added.

Mr. Collins nodded. "I am indeed. My daughter told me the Zucker girls were charging two dollars for a chance to win the big prize."

Caroline's father took a deep breath. "And

you're telling us that you knew nothing about it?"

"That is correct," Mr. Collins answered, scowling.

"You're right—we need to talk," Mr. Zucker said. He saw Caroline in the hallway. "Get your sisters and bring them in here," he said grimly.

Caroline walked slowly down the hall and knocked on Patricia and Vicki's bedroom door. When Patricia opened it, she said, "Samantha's father is here. Dad wants us to come into the living room right away."

Patricia's blue eyes and Vicki's brown ones grew as big as saucers. "Oh, no!" Vicki wailed.

"Do we have to?" Patricia asked.

Caroline didn't say a word. She just nodded. Patricia took one of her hands and Vicki took the other. Silently the sisters walked back down the hall and into the living room.

All three girls squeezed into the big, soft chair by the window. Mr. Zucker looked at his daughters. "Can someone explain what is going on?" he asked.

They all spoke at once.

"We wanted to help Caroline . . ." Vicki said.

"We were selling seeds . . ." Patricia said.

"They didn't know they would have to pay . . ." Caroline added.

Mr. Zucker clapped his hands. "One at a time. Caroline, you're the oldest. Suppose you start."

Caroline swallowed hard and said, "Patricia and Vicki wanted to help me sell my flower seeds. Since not many people wanted them, they gave them away to kids who paid two dollars to enter the drawing for the shopping spree—"

"The *hundred-dollar* shopping spree," Mr. Collins reminded everyone.

"And you let them do this?" Mr. Zucker asked her, frowning.

"I didn't know about it until this afternoon," Caroline told him.

Mrs. Zucker asked, "How many children paid to enter the drawing?"

Patricia replied, "I'm not sure, but we sold all of Caroline's seeds."

Mrs. Zucker turned to Caroline. "Honey, how many packs did you have left?"

"Two hundred and seventeen," Caroline said.

Mr. Zucker had one more question. "How did two hundred and seventeen children know about the drawing?"

"There was a sign on the wall in the lunch room," Caroline said. That was probably what her sisters had been doing in their bedroom Tuesday night—making the sign and cutting up little squares of paper for the drawing.

"We phoned all our friends, and they told *their* friends and their brothers and sisters," Vicki said. She sounded proud.

Patricia said, "We made sure lots of kids knew about it before we even got to school today."

"That was very clever, girls," Mr. Zucker combed through his hair with his fingers. "But you have caused a big problem for Mr. Collins."

Mr. Collins nodded. "I can't cancel the shopping spree. It would ruin my reputation if I tell all those kids there won't be any drawing."

Caroline saw his point. If people thought Mr. Collins was trying to cheat the kids, they would get mad at him and stop shopping at his store.

Then Vicki had an idea. "I know! You can *donate* the toys!"

Patricia added, "Didn't you donate some prizes to our school carnival, Mr. Collins?"

He smiled for the first time. "Young ladies, I don't think you understand. People donate to charities, or to a good cause, like the school carnival. Do you plan to give all the money to a charity or a good cause?"

"We're giving it to Caroline," Vicki told him.

Patricia explained, "She has to send the money to the seed company so she can win a Porta-Tunes."

"I see." Mr. Collins looked at Caroline and she noticed he had light blue eyes, just like Samantha's. "But Caroline, you aren't a charity. You'll be using the money to get something for yourself."

"I know," Caroline said. *She* wasn't the one who was confused. He should be talking to her sisters.

Mr. Zucker turned to Patricia and Vicki. "Do you understand why it isn't right to ask Mr. Collins to give away a hundred dollars' worth of toys?"

Patricia nodded. "Yes, Dad," she mumbled. "Caroline explained the whole thing to us after school today. We know we made a big mistake."

"I only see one solution," Mr. Zucker said at last. "We'll pay for the shopping spree. Right, Marsha?"

Mrs. Zucker's voice was quiet when she said, "Of course. Since our girls are responsible, it's up to us to handle it. I'll write a check right now."

Caroline pinched herself to be sure she wasn't dreaming. She had never expected her parents to pay Mr. Collins all that money. And they hadn't even yelled or anything. How lucky could she and her sisters get? All their problems were over!

As soon as Mr. Collins was gone, Patricia and Vicki headed for the family room to watch television and Caroline started upstairs to do her homework.

Her foot was on the third step when her father called, "Hold it, ladies. We have something to discuss."

Patricia and Vicki and Caroline came back into the living room. *I should have known it was too good to be true,* Caroline thought.

Mr. Zucker surprised them all by saying, "We don't need to discuss the mistakes Patricia and Vicki made. I think you've worried about it enough today."

"Thanks, Dad," Patricia said. "I can't believe how nice you're being about this—I mean, paying Mr. Collins the money and all."

Her father cleared his throat. "About the money. I haven't yet told you what your mother and I have decided."

Caroline hated to ask the question, but someone had to do it. "What are you going to do to Patricia and Vicki?"

"Nothing," he told her. Then he turned to her sisters. "But *you're* going to do something for your mother and me. You are going to pay us back the hundred dollars."

Vicki's mouth fell open. "It'll take us a hundred years!"

Patricia put her arm around her younger sister's shoulder. "It'll be okay. We can work around the house like Caroline did to earn the money for her Roddy Hastings tape."

Vicki pouted. "I don't want to pull weeds out of those old rocks."

"Then you can plant the seeds that Mom

bought from Caroline. Can't she, Mom?" Patricia smiled at their mother.

"That could be one project," Mrs. Zucker agreed.

"And we could sort bottles and cans and stuff for recycling." Patricia was actually beginning to sound excited.

"We could earn the money a lot faster if Caroline helped us," Vicki said.

Patricia's blue eyes narrowed. "Yeah, we sure could!"

"Now wait a minute!" Caroline said. "*I* didn't have anything to do with the shopping spree. Why should I help pay for it?"

Vicki looked up at her very solemnly. "We only did it because we wanted to help you. We sold two hundred and seventeen packs of seeds."

"Without us, you'd never have sold enough to win the Porta-Tunes," Patricia reminded Caroline.

Caroline had to admit that they were right. Her sisters had gotten into trouble because of her. And she'd promised to think of some way to get them *out* of trouble, but she hadn't been able to do it. So it was only fair that she help Patricia and Vicki earn the money. After all, sisters were supposed to stick together.

"Okay," she said at last. "I'll help."

Her mother smiled at her. "That's very nice of you, honey."

73

"Yay!" Vicki shouted, and gave Caroline a big hug.

Patricia hugged her, too. "We can all do jobs for other people in the neighborhood, not just Mom and Dad," she said. "We could make flyers to hand out to everyone on the block, telling them about our business!"

"If you want to make a flyer tonight, I'll make some copies of it tomorrow," Mr. Zucker told the girls.

"Let's do it right now!" Patricia grabbed Vicki by the hand. "Come to our room, Caroline. And bring your markers."

Caroline wished she could get as excited about the idea as Patricia was. But she wasn't looking forward to spending all her free time working to pay off her sisters' huge debt. She would just have to keep reminding herself how grateful she was to Vicki and Patricia for helping her win the Porta-Tunes.

9

EDDY KETT

"I get to give a flyer to Mrs. Heppler," Vicki insisted Saturday morning.

"Go ahead," Caroline told her. For some reason, her sisters were thrilled to be handing out their flyers to all the neighbors.

When Mrs. Heppler opened her door, Vicki smiled and waved a flyer in her face. "Can we do some work for you?"

"What kind of work?" Mrs. Heppler asked loudly over the sound of Billy yelling in the next room.

"Cleaning projects or yard work," Caroline explained.

"I'll have to think about it."

"That's fine," Caroline told their neighbor. "Just call if you have a job for us."

She and her sisters hurried to the next house. In less than three hours, she and Maria were finally going to their etiquette class, and Caroline knew it would be very rude to be late.

Patricia rang Mrs. Simpson's doorbell and offered her a flyer as soon as she opened the door. Patricia told her, "We're looking for ways to help people with their work."

"Isn't that nice," Mrs. Simpson said, taking the flyer. "I like to see young people volunteering to help us senior citizens."

Volunteering? Caroline realized that Mrs. Simpson thought they wanted to work for her for free. She had to correct things fast.

"Uh—Mrs. Simpson, we're not exactly volunteering," she said. "We're looking for jobs so we can earn some money."

"Oh, I see." The woman's smile faded.

Caroline grabbed her sisters by their sweater sleeves and tugged them away from the door. "We have to go now, Mrs. Simpson. But please call us if we can do any little jobs for you."

"Why doesn't she want to pay us?" Vicki asked when they reached the sidewalk.

"Because she's old and stingy," Patricia answered.

'Don't be mean about old people," Caroline told Patricia. "Grandpa Nevelson is old, but we love him, right?"

"Right!" her sisters said together. They had agreed to stop at every single house on the block. Caroline wished she was almost anywhere else that morning, but she couldn't let her little sisters hand out the flyers by themselves. They had helped her when she needed it, and her Porta-Tunes would be arriving any day now.

"It's your turn, Caroline," Patricia told her when they reached the Hawkes' house.

She wondered if Sammy would answer the door again and tell her they still only grew vegetables in their garden. But when the door opened, she was pleased to see Mrs. Hawke.

"Hi! I'm Caroline Zucker. My sisters and I are looking for jobs we can do around the neighborhood to earn some money." Caroline smiled and held up a flyer for Mrs. Hawke to read.

"This is wonderful!" the woman exclaimed. "I can never get all my work done. How would you feel about scrubbing that moldy stuff off the tiles in the children's bathroom? Or would you be interested in cleaning up the mess in our backyard? My boys never want to do that."

"Gee, Mrs. Hawke, I'm afraid we can't stay today and do all that work," Caroline said quickly. "But you can call us next week. Our number is on the flyer." She knew they were supposed to be looking for any work they could find, but Mrs. Hawke's jobs sounded really disgusting. As she and her sisters hurried off down the street, Caroline told them, "Everyone cross your fingers and wish very hard that Mrs. Hawke *never* calls us!"

A little over an hour later, Caroline, Maria and eight other girls were seated around a big table in the American Legion Hall where the etiquette class was being held. Caroline had barely had time to change into a pretty dress and brush her hair. She hoped she didn't look like a person who had spent the morning ringing doorbells and lining up odd jobs.

"We have two new members today, class," the teacher, Mrs. Smith, said. She smiled at Caroline and Maria. "Caroline, will you please stand up and introduce yourself?"

Caroline stood. She felt stiff and awkward. "My name is Caroline Zucker," she said. Then she pointed to Maria who was sitting next to her. "And this is my friend—"

"Thank you, Caroline," Mrs. Smith interrupted. "Please let your friend introduce herself. And by the way, it is impolite to point."

As Maria stood up and said her name, Caroline sat down. She could feel her face turning red. She hadn't been in the class for five minutes, and she'd already done something rude!

Suddenly a boy came running into the room. He skidded to a stop at the end of the table farthest from the teacher. "Hey! You started without me!" he yelled.

Maria and Caroline stared at each other. "Duncan Fairbush!" they whispered at exactly the same time.

"I bet his mom forced him to come," Caroline guessed.

"Would you care to try your entrance again?" Mrs. Smith asked him.

"No." Duncan sat down and put his feet on the empty chair beside him.

"I believe you meant to say *No, thank you.*" The teacher checked her class list. "You must be Duncan Fairbush. And I am Mrs. Smith. We are very pleased to meet you, aren't we, class?"

The group of girls across the table from Caroline and Maria giggled. They had probably never seen anyone as rude as Duncan, Caroline decided.

Mrs. Smith frowned at the gigglers. "Always remember to behave properly, no matter how rude someone is. As long as you are polite, the other person will look silly."

Duncan frowned when he realized that he had made a fool of himself. He took his feet off the empty chair and sat up straight.

"He almost looks human," Maria whispered, and Caroline tried very hard not to laugh.

"Most of these young ladies here know each

other because they have attended this class before, and Maria and Caroline know each other because they are friends," Mrs. Smith went on. "Let's pretend we're at a party and someone arrives who doesn't know any of the other guests."

All eyes turned to Duncan once again.

Duncan pointed at Maria and Caroline. "I know those girls. They're Maria Santiago and Caroline *Yucker* from my school."

Yucker! Caroline wanted to crawl under the table when the other girls smiled. Duncan hadn't called her that stupid name in months!

Mrs. Smith turned to her. "Now, Caroline, you have a chance to demonstrate my theory of polite behavior. Forget that Mr. Fairbush called you a silly name. How would you greet someone who has just arrived at a party?"

As long as Caroline thought of that person as *Duncan,* she couldn't think of anything polite to say to him. Finally, she pretended Michael Hopkins had just walked into the room instead. Smiling, she said sweetly, "I'm so glad you could join us today."

Mrs. Smith clapped her hands. "Very good! Do all of you see what I mean?"

"Yeah!" One of the girls sounded very impressed. "When she ignored the insult and was polite to Duncan, he looked like a jerk!"

The teacher raised her eyebrows. "It is *not* polite to call someone a jerk, Candice. Try to

80

remember that." Then she gave a piece of paper to each student.

"Manners are really very simple. On the paper I've just handed out, you will find a list of 'magic words' that can be used in most situations."

Caroline read her list:

How do you do?
Thank you very much.
No, thank you.
You're welcome.
Excuse me. (Caroline thought Duncan might use that line a lot.)
May I please be excused?
I'm sorry.

"And now let's have some fun," the teacher said.

Duncan glanced around the room and asked, "Where? *Here?*"

Caroline nudged Maria with her elbow. "He's not learning anything at all!"

Apparently Mrs. Smith couldn't think of a polite response to Duncan's question, so she just ignored him. "We're going to play a little game," she said. "Suppose you were skateboarding down a hill and lost control. What would you say when you crashed through someone's hedge and landed in their swimming pool?"

Duncan didn't bother to wave his hand. He

just shouted, "I'd ask for a life preserver because I can't swim!"

"Doesn't hot air make you float?" Maria whispered to Caroline.

Mrs. Smith ignored Duncan again. She turned to a red-haired girl. "Kathy, what would you say?"

"I'd smile and say excuse me."

Caroline raised her hand and wiggled her fingers. When the teacher called on her, she asked, "Couldn't you also say I'm sorry?"

Duncan hooted. "Yucker says that a lot—she's always making humongous mistakes."

Caroline slammed her hand on the table. "I do not!"

"*Please*, children . . ." Mrs. Smith said softly.

Caroline felt her cheeks grow hot again. *"Excuse me!* But how long am I supposed to sit here and let him say mean things about me?"

The teacher turned to the other girls. "How would you young ladies answer Caroline's question?"

Kathy spoke up. "I don't think she should argue with Duncan. I guess he thinks he's pretty funny, but who'd want to be his friend? I'd rather know Caroline."

Everyone glanced in Duncan's direction, but this time he had no smart answer. Caroline knew Kathy was right. Duncan didn't have many friends, except for a few boys who were just like him. For just a moment, Caroline found herself feeling sorry for him!

10

SISTERS STICK TOGETHER

"Do you think we'll win?" Vicki asked her mother a week later. It was Saturday morning, and all the Zuckers had gone to the mall.

"What do you mean?" Mrs. Zucker asked as they walked along the concourse. "Did you and Patricia enter your own names in the drawing for the shopping spree?"

"Of course!" Patricia said. "Before we let anyone buy a chance, we made tickets for ourselves."

"Caroline, too!" Vicki added.

Patricia nodded. "We put your name on *two* pieces of paper," she told Caroline.

"One of you might as well win," Mr. Zucker said. "After all, you're all working hard to pay for the shopping spree."

Caroline groaned. "Don't remind us! We've got enough jobs to keep us busy all afternoon."

"Just be home in time for the picnic," her mother reminded her. "Grandpa Nevelson is coming over and we're going to grill hamburgers in the backyard."

"Look at all the people!" Vicki exclaimed when she saw the crowd of kids in front of We-Love-Toys.

"Let's get closer," Caroline suggested. "I want to be sure we can hear the name when Mr. Collins reads it."

Mr. Collins and Samantha were climbing onto a small platform that had been set in front of the toy store. The crowd grew quiet when they realized the drawing was about to take place.

"Welcome to the We-Love-Toys prize drawing," Mr. Collins said loudly. Everyone clapped and cheered. "And now my daughter will draw the winning name from this box."

Samantha tossed her long blond hair over her shoulders and made a big production of shutting her eyes tight and sticking her hand into the box. She fished around for a long time before she pulled out one piece of paper and handed it to her father.

He unfolded the square of paper and announced, "The shopping spree goes to ... *Frankie Malone.*"

A bunch of boys cheered, and a tall, skinny kid pushed his way toward the platform, yelling, "That's me! I'm Frankie Malone!"

"What a waste," Patricia said with a sigh.

Caroline shook her head. "I know what you mean. He's probably going to get a lot of dumb models and those adventure video games where you blow up people."

"*I'd* get dolls and stuffed animals," Vicki told them.

"I would have gotten one of those big plastic swimming pools," Patricia said. "Can you imagine that in our yard?"

Mr. Zucker put his hand on Caroline's shoulder. "I hate to mention this, but it's time for us to go home."

"So we can get to work," Patricia finished for him.

"*Stop*, Muffie!" Caroline screamed half an hour later. The dog she and Patricia were walking hadn't looked very strong—until she saw a squirrel.

Patricia clapped her hands and shouted, "Shoo, Mr. Squirrel!"

But as the squirrel scurried away from Patricia, Muffie decided to chase it. Caroline thought her arm was going to fall off because the dog was pulling on the leash so hard.

Muffie dragged Caroline off the sidewalk and through the scratchy bushes at the edge of the park. When Caroline was finally able to slow her to a stop, she called to her sisters, "Who said walking a dog was easy?"

"I'm having fun," Vicki panted. She was breathless from running after her sisters and Muffie.

The squirrel ran up the nearest tree. He sat on a branch high over the girls' heads and began scolding. The dog put her front paws on the trunk of the tree and started to bark.

"Let's take this animal home," Caroline told her sisters. Patricia had to help her drag Muffie away from the tree and down the street.

"I like working," Vicki told her sisters after they had been paid by Muffie's owner.

"That's because Muffie wasn't dragging *you* halfway across town," Caroline said. "Who's next?"

Patricia checked her list. "Mrs. Heppler."

"Do you think she'll give us a treat?" Vicki asked hopefully.

"We're going to Mrs. Heppler's to work and get paid," Caroline told her. "You can't ask for food."

Once they were in the Hepplers' house and saw the basement bathroom they were supposed to clean, Caroline knew they wouldn't have time for treats anyway. Looking at the sticky brown mess, she asked Mrs. Heppler, "What did you say happened in here?"

The woman laughed. "You know how curious Billy can be. He wanted to know what would happen if he shook a can of soda and then opened it."

Caroline made a face. "I guess he found out."

"I'm just glad he did it down here instead of in his bedroom or the family room," Billy's mother said cheerfully.

"We're glad, too," Vicki told Mrs. Heppler with a big smile. "Because now we can make lots of money cleaning it up!"

Mrs. Heppler found buckets, detergent, and sponges for the girls. Then she left them alone.

While Caroline poured detergent into a bucket of water, Patricia scowled at the walls and floor. "I think this job is revolting!"

"I don't mind," Vicki said. "I just like being with you guys. You don't always let me help you."

Caroline grinned at her littlest sister. "We're glad you're helping us today."

She set the foaming bucket in the middle of the floor and handed one sponge to Vicki and one to Patricia. "Time to start scrubbing. Ready . . . set . . . go!" They all plunged their sponges into the bucket at the same time.

"Let's have a race," Patricia suggested. "We'll each take a wall and see who gets done first."

"But I'm too short to reach anything," Vicki complained. Caroline lifted her onto the vanity. "Not anymore. You can wash the tiles over the sink."

All the girls started scrubbing so hard that soap bubbles flew through the air. Patricia giggled when some of them landed in her hair. Vicki thought she looked so funny that she scooped up a handful of bubbles and threw them at Caroline. In minutes they were all having a bubble fight. Then they started throwing their sponges at each other until their hair and clothes were soaked.

"I give up!" Patricia cried at last, pushing her damp hair away from her face.

"This is great!" Caroline said. There was soapy water all over the bathroom. "Now all we have to do is mop up the water, and Mrs. Heppler's bathroom will be clean!"

As the girls wiped up the water, Patricia asked Caroline, "Can I borrow your Porta-Tunes when you get it? You know, I *did* sell most of your seeds."

Caroline frowned. "Is that the only reason you did it? Just so you could use my cassette player?"

Patricia blushed a pale shade of pink. "I guess I thought about it . . . a little."

"But we *really* helped you because sisters have to stick together," Vicki said.

Patricia hung her head. "I'm sorry, Caroline. Vicki's right. I mostly helped because that's what we always do for each other."

That made Caroline feel so much better that she threw her arms around both of her sisters. "I love you guys!" she told them.

"I can't believe this!" Patricia complained that evening as she stared at the food on the picnic table. "Mom, do I have to eat *broccoli?*"

Caroline thought about complaining, too. Then she remembered what she had learned in her etiquette class. It was rude to tell the cook you hated part of your dinner. Without a word, she put one small broccoli spear on her paper plate.

"Why, Caroline!" Her mother sounded amazed. "Are you actually going to try some broccoli tonight without an argument?"

Caroline said, "Mrs. Smith told us it was polite to take a teeny bit of everything. Then, if you don't like it, you just leave it on your plate."

"Come and sit by me," Grandpa Nevelson called. He patted a spot on the picnic bench beside him.

"Thank you. I would like that very much," Caroline told her grandfather.

"Watch out for Caroline," Patricia warned

him. "She's practicing her manners stuff on you."

Grandpa Nevelson ruffled Caroline's hair with his big hand. "I don't mind. She can practice on me as much as she likes."

Mr. Zucker was grilling hamburgers over the fire. He told Grandpa Nevelson, "We're very proud of our girls. They've been working together to pay off their debt."

"I've never seen them act so responsibly," Mrs. Zucker added. "They're really growing up."

Caroline beamed. She loved it when her parents said such nice things.

"I've been thinking about that shopping spree. A hundred dollars is a lot of money," Mr. Zucker said.

All three girls nodded in agreement. It was more money than they could imagine, especially since they had earned only ten dollars so far.

"Don't you think Patricia and Vicki have learned a lesson?" he asked Mrs. Zucker and Grandpa Nevelson.

Their mother nodded. "I'm sure they have."

"Since everyone is learning so much and acting so responsibly, I'm willing to make a deal," Mr. Zucker said. "Instead of paying me back the whole hundred dollars, how would you girls feel about paying me twenty-five dollars?"

"Only *twenty-five dollars?*" Caroline couldn't

believe her ears. "I bet we can earn that in one more weekend," she told her sisters.

"Then we won't have to work until we're all in high school!" Patricia cried.

Caroline didn't need to think back to her etiquette class to know what to do next. She hopped off the picnic bench and ran over to her father. Patricia and Vicki followed her, and Baxter followed Vicki.

"Thanks, Dad! We love you!" all three girls cried at once as they threw their arms around him.

"What about me?" Mrs. Zucker asked, laughing.

Mr. Zucker grinned. "Get over here, Marsha. You too, Grandpa!"

Soon the whole family had their arms around each other in a giant hug. Baxter wriggled his way through until he was right in the middle.

Caroline knew that the hamburgers were probably burning, but she didn't care. Not even burned hamburgers and broccoli could spoil this picnic. Caroline Zucker was the luckiest girl in Homestead, Colorado, and she had the best family in the whole wide world!